Dedicated in memory to Papa,
my hero!

Glenn N. Gibson
April 26, 1898 - September 13, 1984

To: Sage

Happy Reading

www.mascotbooks.com

Aggie's Purple Hands

For more information, please contact:
Mascot Books
620 Herndon Parkway, Suite 320
Herndon, VA 20170
info@mascotbooks.com

Library of Congress Control Number: 2018904154

CPSIA Code: PRT0618A
ISBN-13: 978-1-68401-650-1

Printed in the United States

Rhonda K. Gatlin

7-21-19

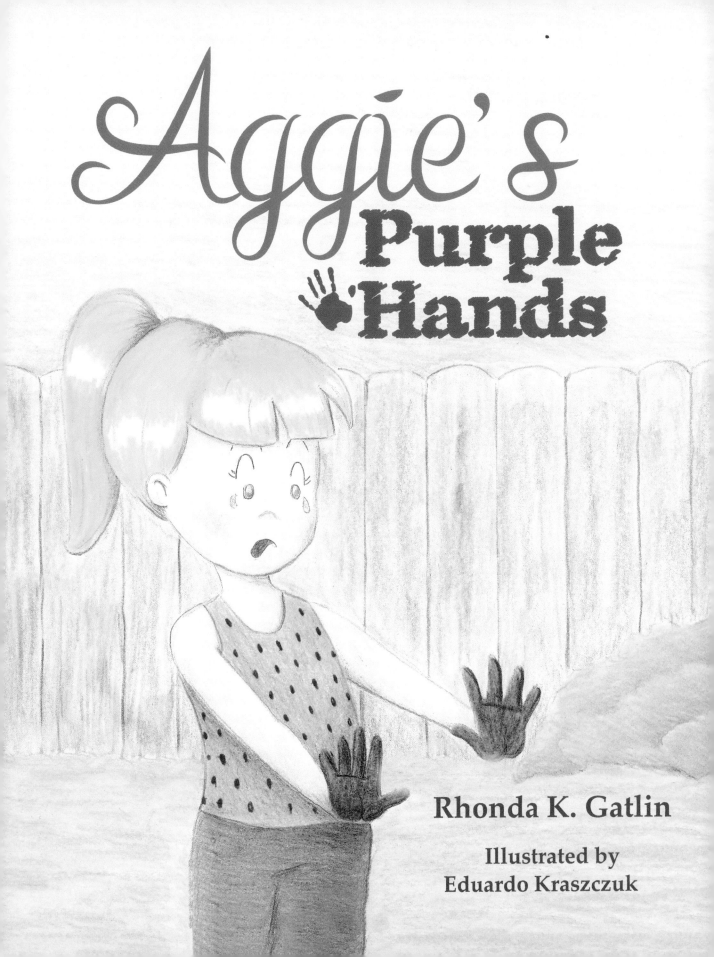

Six-year-old Aggie lived with her momma, daddy, and her four-year-old brother Roger in a small town in southern Alabama. Aggie loved to visit her grandparents with Roger. Granny and Papa lived just down the road from them. Aggie enjoyed helping Granny in the kitchen, and she loved to rock with Papa on the front porch on a lazy afternoon.

Aggie got ready for bed. She was thrilled knowing that she was going to have her first lesson in making jelly at Granny and Papa's house tomorrow. She scooted under the covers, twisting to find her comfortable spot. She smiled, and nodded off to sleep.

Momma's call woke Aggie earlier than usual. "It's time to get up! We have a big day today! We're pickin' grapes and makin' jelly."

Before the fun could begin, everyone had to get dressed and eat breakfast. Aggie dressed in her favorite purple shorts and polka-dot top. The purple reminded her of the yummy grapes she would help pick today.

The smell of bacon wafted through the house. Aggie grabbed Roger's hand and led him into the kitchen, toward the delicious aroma. Momma scrambled the eggs and spread fresh butter on the toast. The family gathered around the table for breakfast.

After Momma washed the dishes, she let them drain in the sink. Then, Aggie and her family walked two blocks down the road to Granny and Papa's house.

In Granny and Papa's backyard stood a big grapevine arbor. Grapes hung down on all sides, making a perfect hiding place for Aggie to play with Roger. They ran for the arbor under the morning's drizzle. Hidden beneath the big grape leaves, they couldn't even tell it was raining.

Roger roared, "I'm captain of the ship. Hand over your gold!" He looked just like a pirate with his black tricorn hat.

Aggie squealed, "Oh, no! I've been captured by Captain Jolly Roger!" Then she snapped her fingers and ran into the house. She knew just what would make the perfect pirate's treasure: Granny's costume jewelry! Aggie filled a shoebox with jewelry for her treasure chest, said a hasty thanks to Granny, and ran back outside.

Aggie bolted under the grapevine arbor with her treasure chest of jewels under her arm. Captain Jolly Roger eyed it with interest, but she held the treasure tight against her side. When he wasn't looking, she laid her treasure chest near the base of the grapevine for safe keeping. She'd come back for it later.

Papa strolled out of the house when the rain stopped. He bent down to see Aggie and Roger under the arbor.

"What are y'all doing?" asked Papa.

"We're pirates," said Roger. "I'm Captain Jolly Roger!"

Aggie puffed out her chest. "I'm the first mate."

Papa saluted. "Permission to come aboard?"

Aggie saluted Papa. "Come aboard, sir!"

Papa saluted and entered the pretend ship.

Papa squatted onto the damp ground under the arbor. Spreading his arms above his head, Papa said, "When I was a little boy, about your age, Aggie, I stood on this very spot helpin' my granddaddy plant this vine."

"It's a tree, Papa," said Roger.

"No, son, that is just a very old grapevine that looks like tree branches. Over the years they've twisted and bent. One of the vines has formed a special seat just for y'all. See how it bends down to fit your size? This type of vine is called a scuppernong grapevine. It grows scuppernong grapes."

"A- a- what kinda' grape, Papa?" asked Aggie.

Papa repeated more slowly, "Scup-per-non'. It mainly grows in the southern United States, sometimes called the Deep South. These vines can live for hundreds of years. This here ol' vine is a baby compared to a vine growin' in North Carolina. That one's over 400 hundred years old."

"Whoa! That's some ol' vine!" cried Aggie.

Aggie picked a grape, bit off the end of it, and peeled back the thick skin. She popped the inside, or pulp, into her mouth. "They taste really good."

Aggie spit out the tiny seeds just as Papa said, "Watch out for those seeds. Careful, you don't want to swallow them. You might grow a grapevine in your belly."

Aggie giggled. "Papa, you're teasin' me."

Papa laughed too. "Yes, honey, I'm teasin' you, but still don't swallow those seeds."

"I won't either," said Roger, spitting his seeds onto the ground.

Aggie's eyes lit up seeing Momma, Daddy, and Granny come out of the house. Daddy carried two big baskets for picking the grapes. Granny  had two smaller baskets for Aggie and Roger. "Many of these grapes are too high for you to reach," said Granny, "but there are enough low-hanging grapes for you two to fill your baskets."

Everyone picked grapes most of the morning. Aggie and Roger took a few breaks, but they managed to fill their baskets.

Aggie held the back door for Daddy so he could bring in the baskets of grapes. Then Papa passed by her and said, "It's time for me to go to work." Aggie loved to see her Papa in his uniform. He worked as a conductor for the railroad.

After Papa changed, he hopped into his truck, a beautiful light blue pickup. Rolling down the window he said, "I'll be back later this afternoon. Y'all behave. Stay out of the kitchen unless you're asked to help. It's hard work makin' jelly."

Aggie peeked through the screen door, eyes wide, and saw the counter covered with Mason jars, funnels, a colander, and cheesecloth. She also saw tongs and ladles for handling the hot jars and liquid.

Aggie watched Momma and Granny washing the grapes and picking off the stems. Momma and Granny shared a wink. Then Momma turned toward the screen door. "Aggie, do you want to help mash the grapes?"

"Sure do!" cried Aggie, running in.

Momma and Granny continued washing the grapes as Aggie opened the screen door.

"We are going to use two different sized jars," explained Daddy. "Let's play a measuring game while Momma and Granny get ready to make jelly."

Daddy brought both jars to the sink along with a measuring cup. "Let's use water for now. Fill that measuring cup and pour it into the smaller jar."

Aggie took the cup, filled it with water, and poured it into the smaller jar. She counted one and filled her cup again and counted two.

"Two cups equal one pint," said Daddy.

Then Aggie went back to the sink with her cup. She poured water into the bigger jar. One, two, three, four times she filled her cup. Daddy said, "Four cups equal one quart. Now let's see how many pints go into a quart."

Aggie filled the pint jar twice.

"Two pints equal one quart," said Daddy. "You and Roger will have your own pint size jar of jelly."

Just then Momma said she was ready for Aggie to help.

Momma put Aggie at the far end of the kitchen table with a small bowl and a potato masher. Aggie climbed onto the kitchen chair and got up on her knees so she was high enough to mash the grapes.

She mashed and mashed and mashed, but the grapes would not stay in the bowl! Every time she pushed down, a grape would pop out and roll onto the table. And every time, she'd scoop it up and toss it back. But they kept popping out, until she came up with a new idea. She asked Momma to cut a hole in a piece of cheesecloth. Aggie put the handle through the cheesecloth to keep them all in the bowl. By and by, she had a bowl of squishy grapes.

Granny and Momma had mashed their grapes, too, and they were ready to put them in the big pot on the stove.

"Honey," Granny said, "you've been a big help, but now it's time for you to go outside and play. The stove is very hot and I don't want you to get burned. The water is boilin' and the kitchen is gettin' steamy. Go outside and get some fresh air for a little while."

Aggie hopped down from her chair and headed toward the door, heartsick. "I'll be back later I guess."

But moments later, Aggie poked her head back in the door. "Just let me watch, Momma, please," she begged. "I'll stay out of the way and be real quiet."

"Oh all right," said Momma. "Come on back."

"This is a perfect time to learn how to make jelly," said Granny. "This big pot filled with mushy grapes is cookin' down to get the pulp and juice for makin' the jelly. The Mason jars and lids are in this pot of boilin' water to make them clean."

Aggie scrambled up onto the high stool to see the entire kitchen.

"When the grape skins fall away from the pulp, it's time to strain the juice," Daddy said, "and that's where I come in." Daddy held the heavy pot so Granny could spoon the grapes into the bowl.

Aggie sat motionless in the steamy kitchen watching and listening to the adults. Momma held the cheesecloth and Granny ladled the steaming hot grapes into the bag.

Then Momma slipped on a pair of rubber gloves. She squeezed the bag to get the juice from the grapes.

Time passed in the steaming kitchen. Sweat dripped down Aggie's nose as she waited to help. Aggie perched her elbows on the kitchen counter, her head hanging down, waiting for something to do.

Granny turned to Aggie. "I need your help. Will you go out to the big garbage can and scrape out these grape hulls? We don't need them to make the jelly, we just need the juice. Then bring back the empty cloth so we can use it again."

"Yipeee!" Aggie cried, jumping off the stool.

Aggie grabbed the cheesecloth bag. It gushed through her fingers and juice dripped down her wrist. Once she reached the garbage can, she scraped the grape hulls from the bag with her hands.

Aggie carried the cheesecloth bag to the back door carefully. She reached for the door handle and screamed. "My hands are purple!" Big tears began trickling down her cheeks.

Granny came to the door to see what all the noise was about. "What is it, Aggie?"

"My hands are purple!" she cried. "I don't want purple hands!"

Granny put her arm around Aggie and led her into the kitchen. Aggie rushed to the sink right away. She scrubbed and she scrubbed and she scrubbed, but they stayed purple. "My hands are purple for life!" she cried.

Later that afternoon, Aggie sat on the back porch waiting for Papa. She hoped Papa could help her when he got home from work. So far, everything she had tried hadn't worked, and her hands were still purple.

When Papa drove into the driveway she hopped up and ran to his truck. Papa climbed out as soon as he saw Aggie. "What's wrong?" he asked, wiping away her tears.

"My hands are purple forever!" cried Aggie.

Papa looked at Aggie's purple hands, picked her up, and gave her a big hug. "I know just what to do."

Papa carried Aggie into the bedroom and pulled out a pair of Granny's white gloves from the dresser. He put them on Aggie's hands and said, "Now you don't have purple hands anymore."

Aggie stared up at Papa for a few seconds, then wiped at the tears drying on her cheeks. Her face spread into a big grin. "No more purple hands!"

Just then, Roger appeared in the doorway. Aggie waved at him with her clean white gloves.

Roger looked up at Papa. "I want some gloves, too."

Papa patted Roger's shoulder and said, "Yes, sir, you do, but let's get you a manly pair of gloves from the garage."

Aggie, Roger, and Papa headed to the garage. Before long, Aggie spied a smaller pair hanging on a hook. She grabbed them, saying, "These are just your size."

Roger looked down at his new gloves. He looked up at Papa and whispered, "I'm manly, just like you."

Aggie smiled at Roger. "We can wear these gloves for the rest of the day."

Roger beamed.

When Aggie peeked back into the kitchen everything was clean. She saw three pint jars and three quart jars sitting on the counter. Each looked like it was filled with Jell-O, but after it was cooked it wasn't purple anymore. It looked almost pink! Her mouth watered at the thought of eating scuppernong jelly on her toast.

Granny put two pint-sized jars of freshly made scuppernong jelly into a brown paper bag. "Hold on tight so you will have jelly for your toast in the mornin'. Be careful on the way back home."

"Thank you, Granny," Aggie said. She held the brown paper bag tightly to her chest with her gloved hands.

On the way home, Aggie's heart thumped, hoping they would be home soon. She slipped in between Momma and Daddy for extra protection for the treasure she now carried. Proud and satisfied, Aggie grinned up at her daddy.

The next morning Aggie woke up excited. She was finally going to try the scuppernong jelly! But as she climbed out of bed, she peeked under her gloves and discovered that her hands were still purple. She was heartbroken.

She quickly pulled her gloves off and rushed to the sink to lather her hands with soap. She washed and washed and washed, then she rubbed and rubbed and rubbed, but the stain wouldn't go away.

Momma came into the bathroom carrying Granny's gloves. She dried Aggie's tear-streaked face and put the gloves back on her hands. "Come on, honey, let's go get some jelly."

Momma steered Aggie toward the breakfast table. There, sitting by her plate, sat a brand new jar of scuppernong jelly. Aggie bounced up and down with delight, forgetting all about her purple hands. She was ready to taste the jelly she helped make. She took a bite. It was so sweet on her tongue. It was delicious! It was scrumptious!

Later that afternoon Aggie walked down to see Granny and Papa. She found them in their rocking chairs on the front porch. She hopped up onto Papa's lap and they rocked back and forth together as Aggie told them how good the scuppernong jelly was.

"I see you're still wearing Granny's gloves," Papa said.

"My hands are still purple," said Aggie, holding up her hands. "I don't want purple hands anymore."

Papa leaned down and whispered into Aggie's ear, "Do you remember last summer when I stained Granny's dresser? I got brown stain on my skin, and it took days for the color to go away. You've got your very own stain from the grapes, Aggie. It will wear off in a few days. If it makes you feel better, just keep wearing the gloves."

Granny leaned in close and said, "Now, Papa, don't be givin' all my gloves away. I need a pair for Sunday."

Aggie and Papa giggled. "Come on, Aggie," said Papa, winking. "Let's go get you a clean pair from inside."

A few mornings later, Aggie woke up, took off her gloves, and looked at her hands. "My hands aren't purple anymore! The stain is gone! Roger, look!"

As Roger appeared in the doorway, Aggie twirled around and around and around, and sang, "I don't have purple hands anymore. I don't have purple hands anymore. I washed it all away!"

She dressed and picked up Granny's gloves. "Momma, may I go see Granny and Papa? I need to tell them about my hands and return Granny's gloves!"

"Yes, sweetie, run along," said Momma.

"I'll see you later."

Aggie rushed down to her grandparents' house. She knocked on the front door. Tapping her foot, she waited for Granny to open the door. When Granny answered the knock Aggie shouted, "No more purple hands! The stain is gone! Thank you for lettin' me borrow your gloves." She gave Granny a big hug and asked, "Where's Papa? I need to tell him, too."

Aggie ran into the living room, hands outstretched and a big grin on her face. "No more purple hands! I washed the stain away!"

Aggie and Papa said together,

"No more purple hands!"

About the Author

Rhonda K. Gatlin's heart and soul is firmly planted in the south. Rhonda was born in Tampa, Florida, attended high school in Montgomery, Alabama, received her Bachelor of Science from Auburn University, and her master's in literary arts from Lesley College. She stayed in the south to teach elementary children for 14 years. Rhonda moved to Boulder City, Nevada, in 1989 where she resides with her husband Chris. Rhonda's son Ryan Osbourn, granddaughter Jade Parker, and grandson Oliver Osbourn live in Alabama where she often visits.

Rhonda retired after teaching an additional 25 years at Andrew J. Mitchell Elementary School in Boulder City, Nevada. In 2016, Rhonda received the American Graduate Champion award from Las Vegas Public Broadcasting System (PBS) for her active role in making a difference in students' lives. She continues to make a difference with children through tutoring and reading aloud in elementary schools.

Also by Rhonda K. Gatlin
Granny's Cobbler: A Counting Book

About the Illustrator

Eduardo Kraszczuk is a Brazilian illustrator and translator. Ever since he was very young, he has loved to draw his favorite cartoons and comic book characters. And the thing is, he never stopped. Nowadays, he loves his work illustrating children's books, surrounded by his beloved books, old PC games, and his adorable (and sometimes annoying) cat Sofia in his home studio where he plots world domination or what to have for lunch. Usually lunch.